I0551702

JOHN

URBANCIK

THE NIGHT
CARNIVAL

John

Urbancik

The Night Carnival

Copyright © 2021 John Urbancik

All rights reserved.

Cover art and Design Copyright © 2021 John Urbancik

Interior Design Copyright © 2021 John Urbancik

This is a work of fiction. Similarities to persons, living or dead, are neither intended nor should be inferred.

For more information, please visit www.darkfluidity.com

ISBN: 978-1-951522-05-6

John Urbancik

The Night Carnival

PART ONE

Yes, I know, this is probably a dream. But you can never be certain. It's night out there, the moon is as full as she's going to get, and none of those lazy drifting clouds threaten rain, so it's a beautiful night. The crisp air smells of honey and fairy floss and funnel cakes, and yes, also pigs and horses.

So come on in, enter, be my guest. I'll personally guide you through the wonders our carnival has on offer. The lights—the colorful lights, the neon signs, the bulbs strung over the midway like flowers—there's nothing uneasy about them, not at all. Trust me, the buzz you hear is pure excitement. If any of the lights flicker, they're supposed to. There's no ghosts—at least, not until we get to the dark rides—and those aren't likely to cause much by way of harm.

So come along, take in the sights, hear the sounds, the music, the screams—of joy, I assure you. This is a joyous place, to let loose with your inner child. I know you've got one inside you. We all do. Some of us have more than one. Take my hand, I'll conduct you through the gate, under the teeth of that grinning clown. I'll admit, we stole that, but a long time ago. This is the Sebastien Brother's Night Carnival, and we're not above a little bit of a thievery now and then. So yes, keep your wallets and purses secure, and your watches, your rings, your souls. Welcome, my friend, to the strangest show.

Don't worry about the ticket counter. I've got you covered. As far as I'm concerned, you've already paid your way in. Here, right at the start, is the kiddie Ferris wheel. Six little cars, round and round they go, not revealing too much. Children are easy to scare, and we don't want that. So they climb in, old Hector will help with the safety rail so they don't fall free. We haven't lost a child, not in that way, in thirty seasons. And yes, down in that direction we have the children's midway, all those games of chance, balloon heads you can fill up with a water pistol, roll-a-ball horses, cotton candy, and of course clowns.

Listen, I'll let you in on a little secret: the clowns are here for the children, so unless you're actually under the age of thirteen, you probably shouldn't give them a second thought. Yeah, they have big feet, and who knows what emotional scars they're hiding underneath all that pancake makeup. It's not like they fill their balloons with the breaths of those poor, innocent children. I haven't heard of a single one who didn't leave all smiles, and maybe better behaved than ever before. I can't say why, but it seems the kiddies learn something of discipline, maybe on that little Ferris wheel, maybe on that tiny carousel. The calliope sounds tinny from here, I'm sure, but it fills their little hearts. You can see it in the sparkle of their eyes, the steadiness of their gaze. It's like *they* have the secrets, not us at all, and maybe they'll reveal them when we're ready.

Anyhow, we don't want to disrupt the children. Let them have their fun. The cornfields are not far away. Maybe you'll enjoy the maze. It's quite simple, actually, hardly a challenge at all. The corn doesn't whisper, that's just the wind. No, it doesn't matter if you don't live in corn country. This is the Night Carnival. We bring our own.

Let's walk up the midway. I don't quite trust the guys who work the corn field maze. I'm not sure they've ever seen a pretty girl they didn't like. They chew straw and drink shine, and personally, I wouldn't trust them with my children, much less my own hide. Look at the way that one smiles. It's downright wicked, nasty, and evil. He ain't never lived in a town, not a good ole American town. There weren't any country fairs where he grew up. Look at all those teeth, too. Perfect, they are. White. Gleaming. Sharp.

On the midway, we've got the games, and I know you want to try your luck. But don't waste your money. The woman at the strongman test, she'll kiss you right on the lips if you bang that clapper all the way to the bell, but her eyes are too green, like pools of emeralds, and if you get too close I'm sure you can see the echoes of other men and women who have rung that bell. They think it's a prize, for only a buck, but she's got fairy blood, they say. She tells fortunes and dances in the light of dawn and offers something to the goddess of rainbows, I can't say what. She's beautiful, in all the ways that matter, I'll give you that, and in quite a few other ways besides. But look at her now, eyeing you like you're one of the prize pigs awaiting judgement. She's carving you into bits in her head, loin and shoulder and hocks and jowls. That's no trick of the light, I believe she truly is salivating. I'll tell you another thing, too, a secret, just between you and I. To earn your trust, you might say. That plank she stands next to, there, at her feet: it's loose. She steps on it to tighten the line. It's easy to ring the bell when the line's taut. But when she's not on it, she doesn't like you enough to let you win that kiss. It ain't a feat of strength. It's all up to her.

The balloons are underinflated, too, so those darts will often bounce off. You get three for a buck, and the prize, if you pop just one of the balloons, ain't even worth that much. It's a toy, a piece of plastic, possibly a choking hazard. Yeah, I know, I don't want to spoil your fun, but you're more likely to win at the ring toss. That, my friend, is purely a game of chance. Of course we have time for you to try a few throws. I told you there'd be money flowing out of them pockets before the night was over, and the night's still very, very young.

Better luck next time. I know, it's all in the wrist, but it's also in the wind speed, and the angle of those glass bottles. You weren't any more likely to win those, but at least you didn't lose a pound of flesh in tossing, right?

Here, this is where you risk the flesh. That wheel, it's not spinning now, but in a little while our world-famous knife thrower, all the way from Brooklyn, will be tossing knives at a volunteer, and I've known him to get close enough to the skin to sheer the shirt of an honest gentleman. I'd hate to be tied up there, spinning ever so gently, the night he has a bad throw. Say he sneezes mid-windup. The wheel is painted red for just such an occasion. You'd be surprised at how often he has to clean it.

Here, we have a line of concession stands. Fried bread, fried apples, fried chicken dipped in cereal, fried chocolate bars, fried butter on a stick. I'm sure it's all delicious, if any of that's your thing. In the back, they've got peanuts, almonds, caramel corn, hot dogs, and ice cream. Freshly spun curly fries. Pretzels in a dozen flavors. And an assortment of finger food, none of which comes from the monkey house. First, we would never use our monkey's fingers, and we would never serve them fried like that. And even if we did, they'd be a lot more expensive. A delicacy, fried monkey fingers. And second, no, those aren't the fingers of fairgoers who stuck them into the monkey's cages to poke and prod our animals. They aren't that vicious — the fairgoers, I mean, and I also mean not *usually*. The occasional mishap is, unfortunately, unavoidable, but the monkeys have got to eat, too, and it's cheaper than special ordering their favorite snacks from that one farm in Iowa, let me tell you.

Of course we can skip the monkey house. I thought that might've been a highlight for you, but I've been wrong before. Once or twice. Not very often. There's a live demonstration of sheep shearing, if you'd prefer. A chicken hatchery, if you'd like. A geranium with green leaves and crimson flowers? Prizes awarded every weekend at every new stop along the way.

Don't look so surprised. The Night Carnival comes like the wind, yes, but it goes to a great many places. We did a show in Boise just last year, and El Paso, despite that it's all just sand and sun during the day. At night, we bring out the wildest, vilest, funnest patrons a carnival ever did have.

Yeah, the kiddie midway has the world's tiniest horse, and the kids can feed it. But here, for the more adult crowd, you might say, we'll let you feed the illustrated man, whose tattoos are practically alive. I've seen him rip a snake right off his bicep because he didn't want to have to face a mongoose on his own. I'm sure I'm misremembering the story, too, because it's not like you get a lot of mongooses when you're on the road. Not here, not in Wichita, not in Copenhagen. Go on, pay another dollar and take a look. I won't force you to buy food. He's ever so gentle, though. Takes it right from your hand without leaving so much as a tooth mark in your palm. I can't say the same about the mermaid, though. She's a bit more feisty, doesn't like when she's not in the water, mostly just lays there in her cage like she's not even alive. I've

never seen so many teeth in one mouth before.
Still, there are people who pay for the privilege.
They try to get close with a guppy or a goldfish,
whatever they're handing out back there that night,
and there was only the one time, in all my
experience, that she took a liking to anyone. It was
a boy, not more than five, I don't remember. She
took him into her cage, sheltered him like her own
child, hissed and bared her fangs. The trainers had
to use their poles. It's a lie, that she's stranded on
dry land like that. She can use that tail like an
alligator. I've seen her propel herself halfway down
the midway in the blink of an eye before someone
got brave enough to wrestle her to a standstill. You
don't want to hear her scream, let me tell you. That
sound will break glass, and maybe bones, and
maybe even hearts, though I can't say for certain
because it's a long time since I've had one of my
own.

I did say there was some more adult fare, did I
not? In that tent, there's a lot of leather, latex, vinyl,
whips and such, gags, blindfolds, a stretching rack,
a bed of nails, rings the likes of which I hesitate to
describe. You have to already have your own
password to get in. From what I understand, it's the
safest, sweetest, most secure tent of the carnival.
They'll take care of you. Good care. They don't
break everyone.

In the very next stall, you'll find the
contortionist. She's like an octopus. Can't keep her
in a cage, a coffin, a chest, nothing. She's an escape

artist, so the handcuffs won't work on her unless she's feeling particularly playful. And she's vindictive. Will take back the key from whatever volunteer was unfortunate enough to be lured into locking her up. I'm not sure she's really got bones beneath that flesh. I've heard she's slipped underneath the cracks of locked doors. Got herself into the trunk of a patron's Toyota one night, stowed away to his home, tied him to the ceiling, and kept breaking bones in his hands and arms and chest until he finally managed to free himself. She said that's how it was done to her. She showed him her ribs. Five, she said, in total, enough so that her heart was always at risk. I'm not sure how he took that, to be honest. I'm not sure he survived the night.

No, no, that's not her peeking out at you now. She won't follow you through the carnival for the rest of the night, not while I'm with you. Anyhow, you didn't drive here in a Toyota, did you? I mean, I saw you walking up to the gate, walking down that dirt road in the darkest corner of your neighborhood, your town, your city. You wouldn't drive a Toyota in a dream, would you?

Moving on, here's the magic show, and there's the burlesque show, and that's the dancing waters. The waters are fun, splendid even, just a bunch of synchronized sprinklers and colored lights and a bit of a smoke show. Yes, it's true, we used to have a Gorgon exhibition on the last night of the show, but she left us a long time ago after some trouble with the authorities in, I want to say, Brookhaven. No, I can't be exactly sure where that is. I'm a guide, not a cartographer, not a mapmaker, not a navigator. Ain't my job, really, to know where we are. And that was well before my time. Just how old do you think I am?

Now we come to the first of the rides, the easy one, the simple one: the carousel. Every horse is hand-carved, but only one can be the Lead Horse, the most gallant and regal of them all, so choose well. We've lost more than I care to count on the carousel. The calliope, all that steam moving through whistles, makes such beautiful music, but it can scar. It's not exactly melodic. It sneaks in under the skin, burrows into your veins like worms, I've seen it happen. And if they don't feed the horses regularly enough—and they can never, really, feed them that often—it's always good to bring an apple or something. They love apples, except for the ones that don't, and then maybe pack a carrot as a backup. I don't think there's ever been a horse, on or off a carousel, that won't eat both apples and carrots. I don't care if they're made of flesh and bone or Philippine mahogany, horses can get quite cranky when they're hungry. I've seen little girls come off the carousel in tears, and little boys get torn right up. Once or twice, I mean. Not all that often. Not every night, and certainly not tonight, I assure you. You're safe—maybe not completely safe, who can guarantee any such thing?—but relatively safe, at the very least, on any of those horses tonight. Look, the one with the red saddle blanket, that one doesn't look hungry anymore at all, it's wearing the satisfied grin of a creature that has just eaten its fill, thank you very much. And the one with the purple reins, that one just looks vaguely bored, don't you think? Daydreaming of running free through Montana, I bet, though I'm sure if we ever released that particular horse onto a field in Montana, it would come running back like we'd just introduced the worst of its nightmares. They're agoraphobic, carousel horses, though you'd never know it. We keep them in place with those drop rods. It seems inhumane, but I assure you, we're actually doing what we can to keep them comfortable. When carousel horses get to flying around all loose and free, galloping from one dream to another like they own the realms, you really better hope you're awake for all that.

Like I said, the carousel is easy, and you're free to take a spin, to listen to the music, to rise and descend in perfect rhythm with the rotation of the machine. There's no great metaphor here. This isn't supposed to describe your life to you, or the world, or the way things are. I mean, maybe it is, I'm no philosopher, I'm just your guide through the wonders of the Night Carnival. To be honest, the horses aren't what I'm most excited to show you.

That's coming up. Later. Don't rush me. I can't walk you through the carousel any faster than our feet can carry us. Magic carpets cost too much and aren't really all that safe. Nothing to hold onto but tassels. They start or stop, and you learn real fast the meaning of words like momentum.

Next, these are the bumper cars. They're safe. Of course they're safe. They're pulling loose electricity from a net in the ceiling, they're little plastic motorized things with meager seatbelts, and though there's a track it's not like you're bound to follow a single prescribed route from beginning to end. In fact, the whole purpose is to ram into your opponents—and in the bumper cars, everyone, especially your closest friends and loved ones, are the opposition. There's no prize for first place, there's no point system to determine winners, there's only the occasional chipped tooth, fractured rib, and broken bone. Electricity is safe, you know, even when it cascades freely like that. The sparks, the buzzes, they're just part of the excitement. And there's even a pit, off all the way back in the corner, so if your vehicle happens to break down while the other drivers are still slamming into everyone and everything they can at full throttle, the carnies will guide you into the pit so they can make the necessary repairs, and they'll generally be good about letting you ride again for free. I've only seen one or two people go into the pit and not come back out, only one or two in any given week, at least, but I'm sure I don't see everything so we can't make any real conclusions based on what I didn't see.

Don't you love this next ride? It's like we sit you

in a metallic diaper suspended from a rounded, paneled ceiling by chains, and send you spinning freely for three, four, five minutes at a time. All that centrifugal force, all that blood rushing to the outsides of bodies, all those wild and reckless screams of *joy*, pure and unadulterated—I don't know how we would funnel that into anything, I can't imagine any way of utilizing that energy for nefarious purposes. We're not conjuring demons or opening portals, and we're certainly not brewing transformative concoctions in the pillar at the center—go on, believe that if you must, I'll allow it. Pretend, if it makes you feel better, we're making potions that will change our patrons into grubs or mealworms or roly-polies or some such thing. You know as well as I how utterly insane that is. You'd be thought a madman, especially outside of your dreams, if you go ranting to the authorities that the Night Carnival is distilling its paying customers to construct centipedes. The way we travel, we don't even have the right kind of flora on hand all the time. How are we supposed to maintain an army of crawlers and creepers when we haven't got anything but angel's trumpets and moonflowers to keep us company?

No, the geranium flowers don't count. Did you see any millipedes or scorpions crawling around inside there? I didn't think so. If they'd been there, I'm sure I would've pointed them out. What kind of guide would I be if I didn't?

The Thunder Bolt, the Tilt-a-Whirl, the Tea

Cups—yes, it's true, they're all designed to disorient you and maybe dislodge your lunch. You don't have to ride. We'll be past them all soon enough. But first, let's stop here, for the highlight of our big rides: the Ferris wheel. Not the kiddie wheel, this one, it rises a hundred feet above the earth and gives you the best bird's eye view you'll ever get of this countryside at night outside of a hot air balloon. The gondolas hold four comfortably, but I've seen the clowns—we have thirteen working on any given night—load into one of those cars, and most of them came back. I think it was a willing sacrifice. One of their own had gotten sick, I bet. It's hard to know, really, how clowns think and operate. They don't have lives like you and I know. They're subject to an entirely different set of rules. When the apocalypse comes—or comes again, depending on who you talk to—they'll be praying to their own set of gods, and I doubt they've got an ounce of compassion left over for the rest of us. Yeah, even me. We're not all friends at the carnival, you realize. We're like any family. We have infighting, we have rivalries, we have forbidden lovers and extraordinary trysts, even generational feuds. Sisters who haven't spoken to each other since the minute after birth. Brothers who will eventually duel to the death to inherit the family name.

You don't understand that, do you? Names are important. Older names are, inherently, more important than fresher names, and usually they get passed down to the firstborn. Traditionally, it's been the eldest son, but even in the carnival we've been breaking with tradition these past few decades, and even longer than that, so you should know for a while, the Sebastien Brothers who brought this carnival and the circus and the traveling Christmas show into reality, conjured these things straight from the recesses of their diseased minds, never fought over the carnival, and between them only had the one daughter who inherited it all—including the name. I mean, this was a long time ago, before my time, she's gone now—I told you about that already, didn't I? That nasty business in Brookhaven, you remember. Names are means of control—but that control works both ways, forward and back, and it's sometimes a very delicate balance.

You don't really want to get into all that, anyhow. We're approaching the back end of the carnival. These are the treats you really want to see, and what I've been most anxious to show you. Yes, there's the roller coaster, that's the last of the thrill rides, but beyond that: the dark rides. The house of mirrors. The ghost tour. The other side of the cornfield maze I told you about earlier. The funhouse.

Yes, yes, one thing at a time. So: the Ferris wheel? Do you want to go for a ride? I know Lance, he's the guy pulling the levers, opening the doors, holding out a hand for all the ladies and little girls, all gallant like a true gentleman. You're not wearing a wristwatch, right? He'll pocket that, and anything else in your pockets. He'll bring us up to the top, slowly, one gondola at a time as he lets in other riders, and from that height—why, you can see the world. All four corners. You can see across the cornfields, all those poor souls lost in the maze, and the creatures waiting to devour them if they make a wrong turn. You can see over the forests, where the ravens seem to be waiting for whatever scraps we leave behind. Stretches of deserts, chasms in the earth, mighty rivers, enormous oceans, distant lost continents. From the top of the Ferris wheel, you can see your own house, and the Taj Mahal, and the Tower of London, and the Jaguar Temple, if you know at all what you're looking for. Victoria Falls, the mouth of the Yangtze, the juncture where the Blue Nile and the White Nile meet.

From the top of this Ferris wheel, you might see ancient keeps still protecting mountain passes in Romania and towers of glass and steel in Chicago. You won't be so high as, say, that building in Dubai, but you'll be higher than you've ever imagined. From there, you'll see secret rendezvous, lovers outside Moroccan cafés, murderers prowling Shanghai temples, ghosts dancing on the rooftop of a nunnery in New Orleans.

I mean, these are some of the things I've seen, just a few of them, the simplest and easiest to explain. In fact, there's no telling what you'll see. Maybe the face of the person you'll marry, or the person who will murder you—or perhaps they're one and the same. Maybe a future, maybe a past, maybe something else, who am I to say? I'm not a fortuneteller. The woman at the strongman test won't tell your fortune, not for any price, though she might on a whim when the mood strikes her.

No, if you want a clear view of your future, of what's likely to happen, you'll need to crawl through the dust, pay the same price as anyone else—even me—and see the red witch in the tent, if she'll see you. She's not always there, though I've never seen her coming or going. In fact, I've never seen her, except those few times she's deigned to reveal some aspect of my own future, and like me you'll be sworn to secrecy. You won't want to tell anyone, not even yourself, what it is she shows you.

I can bring you to her, sure. Her tent is just around the corner, here, where the Night Carnival is darkest, where the strings of lights don't reach, where all neon glow has been extinguished and left behind. You would almost think she's not part of the carnival at all, though she, she or her daughter or her daughter's daughter, has been traveling with the Sebastien Brothers since the beginning. I don't know how old she is, I don't even know if she's real. The whole thing might be an elaborate stage show, like that time with the Gorgon sister that I told you about.

I'll bring you to her, but she might not see you. And even if she does, you might not like what you find. You might want to say a prayer, if you're the praying type, though I can say with some confidence there aren't many gods that will follow you into the red witch's tent. I'll tell you what I know: she was born in Prague, in the old country, one of the oldest countries. Her magic is real, or seems real, and since all this might just be a dream, what harm can there be?

I'll wait for you here. Outside the dark and dusty canvas tent. Don't let its size deceive you. There are countries of graveyards inside, but it's best if you experience it yourself. I'm your guide through the Night Carnival, and I'll be waiting should you emerge wishing to see more, but I cannot walk with you into the tent of the red witch. She has her own ways. Her own requirements. Her own costs.

Step right in. But don't blame me if you don't like what she shows you.

PART TWO

Through the flap of the red witch's tent, as your guide steps away and lets it fall, it takes a moment for your eyes to adjust to the new level of darkness. Gone are the neon lights, and all the ringing and music and roller coastering and screaming of the carnival. Instead, there are the smells of dust, dirt, and decay, a gentle wind rolling across the tombstones, and—yes, granite and marble as far as you can see in all directions. Even the flap of the tent has disappeared.

There's no symmetry among the stones. They're not in straight lines. Many have statues or structures. Some are no bigger than a carry-on bag for an airplane. Others are large enough to hide multiple rooms inside. The sculptures include ravens and angels and cherubs and vases full of fresh flowers. One of these is filled with a spray of red roses. Their scent is picked up on the wind.

"You seem decent enough," a voice says. She sounds old, dry, brisk, like she's had more whiskey and cigarettes than in the fever dreams of Janis Joplin. You don't see her, not yet, maybe not ever. A gray fog rolls through the graves. It swallows the sounds of the world, it obscures the ravens, sparrows, whip-poor-wills, and other psychopomps, though you can see their silhouettes shifting through the thick murk.

"I hate always delivering bad news," the woman says. Her voice comes from a different direction, maybe from above you.

You have questions. She's a seer, a fortune-teller, maybe born with magic flowing through her veins. She might have been an oracle at another time, but even now she's more than merely a carnival psychic. So many questions about your future, your fortunes, your fate and destiny, sit arid on your tongue.

The moon is full, full as she's going to get, and through the sound-swallowing fog you hear snippets of music—no melody, no song, merely a note at a time, a single instrument, maybe first a bass so that you almost don't even notice it, then a flute as if in the hands of the Master of Winds himself, then a violin. All from the minor key. All at the edge of your hearing. All restrained.

"Pay your dollar," she says. "Set the coin on the stone to your left."

The stone is irregular, the top of it mostly sloped one way or another, but there's a spot big enough for a single silver dollar—which you happen to find in your pocket. The edge of the stone is rough and sharp. It bites as you set the coin down. Draws blood from your finger. A drop spills on the coin, another on the stone. It must be a trick of the moonlight, the fog, the incense wafting about you, but your blood looks silvery inside the red witch's tent.

"Now, I'm sure you have questions," she says, deliberately and precisely enunciating every word so that they all come slowly through her throat. "I don't care. You want to know of loves lost, where might they have gone. You want to know who you'll meet and what you'll do, and I'll tell you, though the answer will not be to your liking."

You almost catch a glimpse of her, the red cape she wears, the hood that covers her head, the long locks of dead, gray hair tumbling from it. You don't catch her eyes, not directly, and maybe you're grateful for that. Even the fleeting whisper of a glimpse feels like razors scratching your soul.

"You'll wake, one morning, and find yourself alone," the red witch says. "Or you'll believe yourself to be alone, which is the exact same thing. You'll question the things you did, the things you didn't do, your regrets and failings, just as all of us, in time, must. But what you want to know, what you're dying to know, the question that is burning deep within your spirit, is when this will happen, and what can you do to avoid it."

She pauses. Her robes seem to flutter in the wind. You're walking through the graves to keep up with her, so her words don't get lost. She's moving in a direction, maybe a particular direction, but it's hard to know where or why. You notice names on the graves, and you begin to recognize them.

Behind you now, she says, "You can do nothing to avoid it. You have a date with the reaper, with the lady of death, with the charred skull, with the eater of breath. Nothing you do, nothing you say, no amount of money, no amount of pleading, will change this."

This isn't what you want to hear, what you came into her tent for.

"You thought I'd promise happy days and pleasant dreams, prosperity and joy and contentment," she says, "but these are not the things I promise. This is not why people come to see the red witch."

Quite suddenly, you do see her eyes. Amber eyes shaped like a cat's under the shadow of that red hood. Old eyes, ancient, barren, which perhaps witnessed the Sphinx built in Egypt, the wall built in China, nations and empires crumble. She lunges toward you, those eyes burrowing into you so you can't even consider evasion. She grabs your arm, pulls your palm toward her. Her hands are leathery, cracked, pale, cold like death itself. She examines the lines in your hand, she grins with crooked teeth you can barely see in the shadows, and slowly, she shakes her head.

"I see you, and you again," she says.

"I see a bargain you shouldn't make."

"I see a wicked smile, but he is not your friend."

"I see the corn."

"And I see a porcelain mask."

She releases your hand, thrusts it back at you as though she's disgusted by the feel or sense of it. "Nothing else," she snaps. "I see no more. Now go, go back the way you came, before the spiders get too hungry, before the wolves lose their fear, before the moon herself takes an interest in one or more of your destinies."

Then she thrusts a card at you, something like a tarot card. "Take this," she says.

You look at the image. "What does it mean?" you ask. The card is labeled *Thief,* and features an exaggerated art nouveau pickpocket carrying a wallet and walking away from a pair of gentlemen descending unaware deeper into the card.

"Nothing," she says. You've lost sight of her. "It's a souvenir. Enjoy the *carnival.*"

PART THREE

I was beginning to think you wouldn't come out. Was about to cut my losses and follow the path back to the gate, wait for the next hapless dreamer, the next lonely heart, the next scoundrel, rogue, vagabond, criminal, or naïvely optimistic—well, it hardly matters, you're still here, and I'm sure you don't want to talk about whatever she told you. It's yours to keep, to use, to fondle as you try to sleep again.

On to the roller coaster. We call it the Spider Dragon. The rails are the bones of dragons and everything is tied together with spider silk. Hey, I don't make up the stories, I'm just telling you like it is. Come closer, look at the shape of this, no, it's safe to cross that barrier here, with me. I'm not going to lead you into something that'll take your head off. Who do you think I am, anyway?

Touch this part of the coaster's skeleton, right here, this cold piece of metal. That's not metal, is it? Feels smooth like ceramic, doesn't it? But you wouldn't want to use ceramics to hold together a death-defying machine like this. All those drops and spins and loops, you get one crack in the ceramic and you'd have a veritable catastrophe on your hands. No, you want something solid, and what can be more solid than the bones of creatures that require a hundred strong men and a half dozen bona fide heroes to bring down?

Yet in all the years, all of them from the start, there's never been a single strut or rail that's cracked and broken, never a coaster thrown, never an unnecessary decapitation. Shush. I know what I said.

Yes, this ramshackle shack, this thing that's falling in on itself, that seems to be propped up against the souls of the damned—it's the ghost tour, as promised. It doesn't look like much, but you know how looks deceive. There's Jerry now, up on the roof. He's the ghost wrangler. It's his job to keep the ghosts in. The new ones, I mean. A lot of the spirits have been touring with the Sebastien Brothers from the early days, but some were just happy go-lucky patrons like you who were terrible at following directions. Keep your hands inside the vehicles, they always tell you—but someone's always got to reach out, and sometimes they get snatched—by something, someone, somehow— and often eaten alive, mangled, manhandled, and misused. We take care of their bodies in all the most proper ways, of course, but when it comes to their ghosts, well, Jerry's got his hands full. Every night, there's at least one that gets away, albeit just for a short time. He's good at his job. And every night, there's at least one newcomer, one ghost we didn't have to feed the night before. That always makes his job harder, but it's the part he likes best. I think he finds a certain joy, maybe glee, in rounding up new batches of spirits for use in the dark rides.

Not all the ghosts are made to work the ghost tour. We can go in if you'd like. I can't guarantee anything. This deep in the carnival, it's really a matter of intelligence and common sense. There ain't no covenants they've got to follow prescribing that they don't scare, tickle, or cut you. They're supposed to be spooky, and I guess some of them think the reek of death, the hint that this may be your last breath, really makes the ghost tour something special.

Look, Jerry's waving. He's happy to see you, I bet. He can tell at a glance whose bodies contain good spirits. By good, I don't mean you're a good person—I'm not your conscience, and such things have no place in a carnival of any sort—I mean a meaty, substantial spectral presence trapped within that skin of yours.

Maybe we shouldn't get too close. He looks hungry, and there are still things I haven't shown you. We can visit him after, if you're still able and willing. Maybe by then he'll have found a meal for the night and you'll be—well, *safer*.

I never promised safe, did I? I think you misheard me, or misunderstood, or took something I said to mean more than it does. If I said we'd be safe at any point, clearly I misspoke. It's not the worst thing I've ever done in my life. Hell, it's not the worst thing I'll do tonight.

The moon has drifted quite a bit since we

began this tour, and there's so much still to see before the finale, so let's move along. We have to go into the funhouse. There's no choice. It's an adventure, it is, and who doesn't love a grand adventure?

People love the bright colors and lively sounds. It starts simple, just a quick little ladder, and off we go into the heart of the beast. These cylinders are meant to make you dizzy, so keep your feet under you even when the ground shifts. You don't want to slip and fall here. You might break something.

Careful. Here, hold my hand, I'll try to keep you steady. You almost fell in. Those trapdoors are obvious, if you're looking for them, but I suppose I should've warned you first. Hey, it's not the end of the world or anything. We've got more to see.

Watch out for the walls here. Sure, they push in and out rather gently, but one or two of them—I can never remember exactly where or how many— are spiked, even if those spikes are rather small. One drop of blood might spark a frenzy of sorts. You don't see them, but the clowns are watching you—watching us, to be perfectly honest—and they've got three rows of teeth just like sharks.

Grab that rope. Pull yourself up. It's easy, nothing to it, but you better be quick. Here, I can help—but just this once. It's not my job to keep you safe. I'm just a guide. I'm not here for your amusement, but to make sure you get from beginning to end or die trying.

Hehe. Yeah, it's just a little joke I tell all the rubes.

No, no, I mean nothing by it. I know you're way more sophisticated than our average victims—I mean, of course, patrons. Watch your step in here, those drops to either side are not well cared for. At least the webbing will break your fall. I'm not sure you'll appreciate it, though. Sometimes, a quick end is better.

Duck!

Wow, that was close. I almost forgot. Well, the funhouse *is* certainly fun for the designers. I'm not sure they ever had you in mind. Here, it's over, just step on through this black velvet curtain—of course I mean it, I haven't lied to you yet.

Okay, yeah, this is another of those cylinders, but pitch black. All the light that tries to get in gets sucked away through little vacuums set at ankle height. No, I can't explain the physics. Whatever you feel at your feet, just keep pushing forward, it's not likely to trip you up. If someone takes your hand—that's not me, won't be me, not at this stage. Don't follow her. Don't even follow my voice. Keep your head and move your feet forward. Sound can echo in here, trick you, lead you astray. Think of the fairy woods, where will-o'-the-wisps will promise safety and warmth and light, but then pull away the veil at the last moment to reveal another rotten tree stump, another broken tea set. Not even a drop, don't even touch those herbs, haven't you been listening to the fairy tales? Anyway, that's where she'll lead you, no matter how soft her urgency appears to be. Straight through is the only way. Ignore the grasping hands. Ignore the whisperings. Empty promises, pale threats, nothing is real in this last room, nothing but you and I and the funhouse itself and the stars outside, if you ever see them again.

The moon sure is bright after the funhouse, isn't it? Don't stray from the moonlit path ahead of us. It ambles to one side and another, but that's the way of moonlight. It sways. It dances. Think of it as ballroom, you and your partner the moon, or maybe something a bit more suggestive. A tango, perhaps? If I had but one rose, I would present it to you here, you could clutch it between your teeth as you woo the moon. She's taken quite a liking to you, I see. The path is crisp between the funhouse and the house of mirrors.

That's a highlight.

Look, it's a glass building, and we haven't ever lost a soul within. Each has been accounted for. Remember, Jerry's been busy collecting ghosts.

And no, there's really no going back. You can't go in the out-door, not in the funhouse. You'd never make it through the darkness. You'll be sipping tea with the fae folk. Not the kind who grant wishes. They may tell stories of you later, I don't know, that depends on your level of gallantry, your courage, your ability.

It's all just glass walls, and the mirrors will make you look—well, maybe more like you, maybe less, but ultimately they're liars, remember that. I'm not allowed in after what happened last time. One word of advice: don't break anything.

Yes, I can still see you. You're doing fine. No, you'd better turn right there. To the left—you've heard of the minotaur, right? Half man, half bull, trapped in the labyrinth and fed an endless supply of failed and inadequate suitors? Maybe I get my stories confused. The important part to remember is Icarus, with the wings. No, the important part is—well, you don't really have time to dawdle. Stop admiring your squat, shortened reflection. Remember the tale of Narcissus, cursed by staring too long at his own quite lovely features. Loved by an echo, a mere echo, practically nothing, and why? Can you tell me that? You can't, can you?

Better turn right there. You're getting closer. Those reflections, they're trying to trick you. That's not really an image of you at the age of six, that's not your first kiss—no, seriously, if you get caught there you'll learn the truth about the succubus and incubus legends associated with the Sebastien Brothers. Even before that fateful night in Brookhaven, the Greek pantheon had swept through the carnival and left their marks everywhere.

Yes, yes, that's you with all your sins revealed on the outside. An ugly sight, isn't it, Dorian Gray? Now keep moving. Can you feel the breath of the bull behind you? Makes me nervous, it does, and I'm not the one at risk.

Oh, no, that was a wrong turn. Yeah, you're stuck now, I can see the glass and mirror walls shifting, adjusting, compensating for your poor judgements.

Don't panic. And don't run. You can't apply logic inside the mirrors. Everything gets doubled back and turned over in reflection. When I said go left, you should've gone right. When I said the minotaur was behind you, I meant ahead of you. Of course it's a trap, but it's also a test, and I really expected you to pass this one.

Yes, those do appear to be sensible shoes. But you can't fight the beast.

Ah, but you can break the glass wall. Good thinking. When I'd said don't break anything, I was giving you the hint you needed. Careful, that glass is still sharp, and each of those shards of mirror are now trying to suck your soul into them. Look down as you step over them, but only briefly, and see little versions of you beckoning, pleading, threatening, dreaming. Tis but a dream within a dream within a dream, at this point—but still, be quick in your escape, lest the minotaur catch you or gouge you or consume you.

Welcome to the other side of the mirror maze. Yes, of course I'm going to bow grandly. It's part of my job description. No, we haven't got a lot of time for a breather, but I'll let you sit for a ten count, if that will help. The moon, she still lights our path, and it's straight through the cornfield maze to the freak show.

Might not be what you expect. We have ladies swallowing swords and gentlemen with flippers instead of hands. We have—yes, we passed one or two at the front—but these are the truly spectacular, wondrous, and special specimens. Gathered from across the four corners and everywhere between. You can see their former homes, whether lost, abandoned, or stolen, from the top of the Ferris wheel. An extraordinary machine, that. Will even protect you from the lowest levels of lightning, if the weather's right.

Anyhow, the corn awaits. No, the corn won't eat you. The stalks don't lean into the path as we walk. It's just corn. The leaves aren't razor sharp. The kernels aren't blood-stained, that's simply a trick of the light, of circumstances, of your imagination.

Let's go this way. The moon doesn't care, and I'm fairly sure I hear chewing coming from that direction. The jack-o-lanterns are smiling, that must be a good sign. You can say grinning, but there's nothing inherently wicked about a pumpkin whose seeds have been scooped from its head to make room for a single hand-dipped candle evoking servants of devils and demons who dance for the red witch's pleasure.

You need to grow corn if you're going to have popcorn, and that's almost required in a carnival, don't you think? Right behind candied apples and funnel cakes?

Ah, now, maybe we should backtrack a little. We don't really want to be caught spying upon a shudder of clowns like that. Yes, a shudder. Don't you know your collective nouns? A murder of crows, an unkindness of ravens, an inconvenience of vampires, and a shudder of clowns. They make me shudder. Look at all those big red feet, those noses, the ruffles, all red to hide the blood of sacrifice and, though they might not take me, I'm part of the carnival, I'm sure they'd string you up right here in the cornfield, in full sight of the Ferris wheel, and no one will ever find their way to you. One drop at a time, they'll take your blood—oh, look at your finger, the red witch has already claimed the first drop. Ah, you should've told me that. The clowns must have already scented you.

Quick, this way. Yes, here we run. The moon won't care if you die today or tomorrow or a thousand years from now, she gets what she wants no matter what. Just don't fall into the corn.

Here, on the other side now, we've got a bit of empty field before the trailers that house the freaks. They're not like us, trust me. They're suspicious of outsiders, and even after all these years I'm an outsider to them. I've never been a conjoined twin, I've never been mistaken for a jointed doll, I've never even had a beard like Lucy, and I'm neither a dwarf nor a giant, no matter how tall and thin I may appear to you. I can't walk on stilts, I have only the most modest of tattoos and they certainly don't dance, and although I've tried eating them once or twice, I have no real taste for lightbulbs, glowing or not.

We'll just walk through like we're just walking through, which is really all we're doing. Used to be a different kind of place, when the man running the joint would gather anyone and everyone he could take advantage of, and use them to take advantage of the good public. The Sebastien Brothers were never like that, though. They were always warm, welcoming, a real family, but even they weren't perfect. I wasn't alive then, so I don't know, I can't really tell the stories—but the red witch was there from the start, she and her conjoined twin, separated at the age of sixty-nine, don't ask me why.

She didn't tell you that? Well, you only just met. How can you expect her to tell you her full life's story? I mean, that separation, I hear it was ugly, bloody, full of screaming and cursing, and curses were tossed about all willy-nilly, and maybe a dozen goats died and all the fields within a dozen miles lost their crops. Again, before my time. Yes, I've been with the carnival a long time. I told you the red witch is older than she looks.

He's going to challenge you. He's shadowing your steps, eating nails, glaring at you. Ignore him, like he's ignoring me. Go on. It's not impossible.

Have the twin contortionists caught your eye? They're not a brother sister act. They've been together only since they joined the carnival some half dozen years back. You should hear them bicker, when they're not twisted around each other like pretzels. Always at it, like that's what fuels their love—that, and their shared taste for forbidden flesh, if you get my meaning. No, not your first thought. Keep your mind clean here. They'd be in the leather tent I showed you earlier, if that was their inclination.

Used to be, a man who couldn't hear, couldn't speak, he'd be considered a freak and ridden around from town to town so the old man could charge a nickel for a peep. A dime, and you could ask your questions, anything you like, because he couldn't possibly answer. Or a black woman birthing albino children. It was horrific, the reasons they used to call people freaks. Not here. In our show, they all take on the title themselves, embrace it, live the life.

But ignore the guy chewing nails. Yes, those are thick and long shanks of iron, and I'm sure more than one has been used to kill a man, but he's just trying to intimidate you. There are other things to worry about. Most of the freaks are just regular people with special skills and talents. Fire breathers. Knife swallowers. Acrobats and gymnasts. Not all of them look like their skin's been pickled. Not all of them have scars in the shapes of nations on their backs. Not all of them have eight eyes like spiders or an extra arm or gills.

Oh, did you think we were at the end of the carnival? Yeah, maybe for most people, for the paying patrons who come in with their children seeking good memories to bring back to their happy little homes. But that's not you tonight, is it?

So we're going deeper. Beyond the midway, beyond the thrill rides, beyond the freaks and the mirrors and the maze of corn. I'm going to show you some of the things we don't show everyone. While the carnival is always on the move, one week in Dothan, the next in Tuscaloosa, the next in Casper, Wyoming, you should know it's not every night we're able to set up camp inside a dreaming mind. On such occasions, we're able to pull out all the stops, set up all the rides, and most importantly, peruse through the non-traveling portion of our show. Some of the wagons on the other side of these trees are as old as the sky, and even I don't know what will be inside when I open some of the doors. It's a carnival of magic, mystery, romance, and passion, in equal parts—but not in equal parts for everyone. Most of the children, they only see the magic. Teenagers might find the romance, I can't always say, their minds are usually a jumbled mess. There's an audience for all aspects of the Night Carnival, or it would've closed up shop long ago.

Here we are, at the first of the wagons. As you can see, the spiders have tied it down tight. It ain't going anywhere. No, there's not a lot of room, but there doesn't need to be. The exhibit isn't open to the public. Not just anyone can see what's inside. But you—yes, you've been invited. Allow me to get the door.

See, it doesn't look like much. Dust and memories. Cheap wood airplanes powered by rubber bands. Mason jars filled with the corpses of rats and squirrels suspended in—I can't say what that liquid is, but it smells something awful, doesn't it? Those are old maps, accurate maps to the best of my knowledge, and the sextant, the telescope, even the chronometer were actually lost at sea and recovered only through the efforts of true heroes, many of whom died to bring these and other prizes back to us. That thing that looks like a Mayan plane? It's a bird, and it's real gold, and if you touch it I'm sure you'll be taking someone uninvited home for breakfast.

Don't take too much time to look around. It's all old stuff, but there are no stories behind most of it, nothing we can use in the carnival. We do have quite the collection. Those encyclopedias are great. If you pull out the S volume, it'll tell you, under the heading for *Space*, that if such a trip were possible it would take twenty-eight days to fly an airplane to the moon. And you and I both know the moon is watching us, even now, even though the windows on the side of this wagon are so small. She has vision like you wouldn't believe. She sees all the things. Around the corners. Into hearts. She knows when a woman lies, when a man cheats, when a band has played all three chords in their repertoire. And if she can see us, there's no way it could take that long to fly to her, isn't that right? There's a plane in a dirt runway not far from here, we can always take it up and test the theory, if you want, if you've got the skills to get a Cessna Bobcat up in the air and back down again. I don't know how well she flies, so you'll need to bring some mechanical skills as well as piloting, but the Bobcat comes from an age of daring experimentation, so I'm sure it won't be a problem.

Into the next wagon, then. More old things. Clown things. Clown masks, dried up pancake. That broom was used by a famous clown, I can't remember his name, but you would know him. It's not a magic broom, or a witch's broom. It won't fly you from here to any other place. But if you pick it up—I don't recommend that you do—you'll disturb the resting spirits of a thousand clowns. Once disturbed, they'll pursue you, all stuffed into a single 1956 Beetle complete with twin chrome tailpipes. You can see the skeleton of the Bug itself just beyond the wagon, there, rusted down to nothing, held together by inertia and air pressure. When the ghost of that car gets going, it's blue like Caribbean skies, like powder and nitroglycerin, like the eyes of a lover lost and returned from hell for your soul.

So, as I was saying, don't touch the broom. Or the flower there, that will squirt you, and maybe you'll never be dry again. And that horn, don't squeeze the bulb at the end. It's one of those sounds you just can't get out of your head again, not until you've slept—and since this is all but a dream for you, my friend, we don't want to discover what might happen to your fragile little psyche if we do that, do we?

Okay, out of the clown car before someone finds us here. It's not that we can't be here, it's just that we shouldn't. You can understand that, can't you? Anyway, here, this is an interesting little trailer. I know, it looks like rows and rows of file cabinets—and that is, essentially, what it is. But look, here, inside this cabinet: a trumpet. I bet you weren't expecting that, were you? Go on, open another, see what's inside. Oh, now that's a nice knife, don't you think? Steel and sharp. I believe that's been hand-carved. It's not old, there's not much by way of story attached to it, not that I know. Made by a fierce blonde woman in Colorado, she used it to kill a man—just the one—and I'm not saying he deserved it or didn't, I'm just saying she felt immensely justified and the jury agreed. It's a nice little sheath, too, fancy leather, again made by hand. You should keep that. Go on. Slip it in your pocket. I won't say a word. Your secret is safe with me.

But no, I don't see any reason to keep the trumpet. I mean, I'm not a musical type, it wouldn't do me any good, and it's not something we can slip into a random pocket. Anyone with eyes would see you carrying a trumpet, and anyone with knowledge will know it's this one, and where it came from, and who played it last—no, not Louis Armstrong, though that would be a nice story, wouldn't it?

I love the files, because there's always something different. Here, look: a black cloth bag filled with—oh, shrunken heads. Look, this one almost looks like you. Same hair. Same eyes. I'm not sure the proportions are right, but maybe that kind of thing gets ruined during the shrinking process? I'm not familiar enough to know. They smell of onion, I'd say. I wasn't expecting that. Anyhow, open another, see what you find.

Oh, wow, that's an original contract—one soul, in exchange for a little bit of murder and mayhem, and it's signed and countersigned. That's a binding contract. No, I don't recognize the signatures. You think you do? Maybe you do. I don't know. Signatures are distinct, especially for those artistic types—that looks like an artist's signature, for sure. Maybe a guitarist, a painter, possibly even a poet. They're always feeling too much. Yeah, skimming through this, that's a particularly brutal method being invoked, a thousand needles applied one at a time until the victim finally bleeds out—that's a slow, agonizing death, and I wouldn't wish it on anyone, especially not you. Best to put that contract back. Don't even look at the name of the target. You don't really want to carry that knowledge through the waking world for the rest of your life, do you? What if it's someone you know? What if it's you?

Oh, the next trailer is a fun one. Go on, step inside. There's no one and nothing here that will hurt you, I guarantee it. Just a wall full of masks. Yes, wood masks from Africa, porcelain masks from Venice, they say that leather mask was worn by the

Marquis de Sade, though I find it highly unlikely such masks were easy to come by when he was writing his *Philosophy in the Bedroom*. This mask here, the very mask used in the filming of *Halloween*, though there's no reason to believe that particular lipstick kiss shows the lips of Jamie Lee Curtis. Probably, it came after, well after, maybe even when it was already in this trailer. We get a lot of special visitors, you're not the first and you won't be the last.

Honestly, I give this tour at least once every night. If I can give the full tour, or at least most of it, there's not generally time to start another. But sometimes we lose our guests in the kiddie section. They screw with the clowns, they misunderstand the power of a four year old with a blue balloon, they taste the lemonade. It's the sugar, I'm sure of it. It's just enough for a child of nine, but any older, it starts to become a problem. Attracts the fruit flies, and then the fruit bats, and then the vampire bats, and then...well, I think you get the idea.

Last night's guest? Was lovely, I assure you, and made it all the way to the end, just as I'm sure you will. Most do. Trust me. I'm like a doctor, when I say something like that. Honest and trustworthy and cleaner than whistles, than lollipops, than any baby's bottom. You'd be shocked how many babies people bring to the carnival. This isn't a place for infants.

Oh, last night's guest—rode the Ferris wheel, and I think that's about where they realized the full breadth of the Night Carnival, where they understood the legacy of the Sebastien Brothers. It's a lesson you're still learning, and it's important that you do so, because we're almost at the end.

I wouldn't recommend touching that—I don't care what the red witch told you, I don't want to know, that mask has a dangerous history. So you'll pick it up anyhow. Fine. It survived the Black Death. I don't know if it's still got traces of the disease on it, maybe just enough to drive a person mad. Sure, put it on if you must, you're not listening to me, anyway, though you should see how it makes your nose look.

It's from the festival, of course, the *Carnivale*. It's porcelain, and that's probably real gold and real crimson—by which I mean kermes dyes, or their dried and crushed bodies. Only the females, of course, because they're the ones that produce the dye. It's elaborate, sure, but not any more so than other such masks.

You'll have to get it off yourself. There's nothing I can do to help. I can see you've untied it, you don't have to raise your voice. I've found these things happen naturally. In good course. Calm down a little, breathe, relax, close your eyes and meditate if it'll make you feel better. Because what we see on the other side of this trailer has been decided by you, and nothing I say or do can change that.

In olden times, the masks meant you were anonymous, and you could dress as you'd like, and no one would know your class. You might be a beggar or a prince, but as long as you wear the mask you're not permitted to gamble. Sorry, the Great Council made the rules, not I. As we step outside, please accept this one warning from me, as I'm unlikely to give you any others: do not accept an egg.

See the lights, the stages, the dances, the gambling dens and saloons and, yes, that's a plague doctor there, though I wouldn't get too close. They're as likely to deliver plagues as cure them, and those women with their masks covering half their faces make illicit promises to anyone willing to part with a dollar. Some of those masks have pearls and rubies, and are maybe worth more than you've earned in a lifetime, but don't think to steal one of them, not off the face of an anonymous stranger. You never know if they'll remove their mask to reveal the features of a clown underneath, and then what would you do?

Yes, there are plays, but they're all in Italian, and worse, bad Italian, by players who have memorized the sounds instead of the words. They have no idea of the meaning, and therefore express none of the emotion. But some of them hide the fact that they are, in fact, poets, and their emotions run deep, and I wouldn't trust them, anyhow.

Walk around a bit. Eavesdrop on some of the conversations. There's people speaking languages you know, of that I'm sure. They might be passing secrets to each other, telling stories, revealing true loves, making declaratory statements of the ilk you would not typically make to complete strangers.

Although maybe they're not all strangers. Maybe you know some of the people under these masks. Maybe they're friends, lovers past present and future, enemies, business partners. It's not for me to say. Do you recognize the shapes of people well enough to know who they are without a hint of their face? You might easily be mistaken about any or all of them.

I said do *not* accept an egg. Look, you've just promised that young—or old, there's no way to know—man or woman that you'll meet them for a tryst before the carnival is over. Did you mean to do that? What's inside, anyhow? That's the trick of the eggs: they're hollowed out, and the insides replaced with—often, rose water, and it does smell quite nice, but that looks like ink, quite a nice ink, too, if you happen to be carrying a fountain pen. So maybe it wasn't amorously intended, but still, you've accepted the invitation, and it's dangerous to refuse it.

The court is filled with intrigue tonight. You can feel it in the air, taste it even, all under the watchful eye of our Mistress Moon. Oh, you haven't met her yet, have you? We'll get there, presumably, before the night is done. And yes, it's almost done. I can feel the warmth of that first line of red in the eastern sky, that first scratch of dawn.

It's coming—with all the inevitability of death, it's most certainly coming. We should start to get you back home, though there's still so much more to see and do and discuss. And there's the matter of your friend. We'd better take care of that first.

Here, where the shadows run deepest, I'll leave you to handle your own affairs. I won't be but a shout's length away, here where the moon still shines in all her glory. Be careful, though, and don't agree to anything.

PART FOUR

The shadows crowd thickly about you. It's not just the moon that's hidden, but the colorful strings of light, the torches, the fire pits, even the sparkling reflections of the other *Carnivale* masks. It's the side of a temporary structure, a façade that will later be collapsed, loaded into a truck, and carted to another city a hundred miles away in a procession of old trucks and wagons that maybe have no business traveling the same roads as the rest of us. Maybe they do.

The figure comes up behind you, tall and elegant, lean, sillowy, androgynous behind that leathery mask. You barely had time to notice before, and even now, in the shadow and murk behind the festivities—you can still hear the music, the dancing, the laughter—even now, you can't get a complete visual of the mask. It doesn't cover the full face, leaving the chin exposed, just a part of the nose, and those lips—they're delicate, they're robust, they're neither definitely male or female. And when the figure speaks, the voice plays on the shallow side of depth, giving you no clues as to the identity of the wearer.

"You caught my egg, my prize, my gift," says the figure.

You offer it back. "It wasn't my intention."

"Sometimes, intention is the least important thing there is."

"Sometimes," you say, maybe just to be contrary, "it's the only thing."

It's a burgundy leather, the mask, etched with amazing detail, so that it looks like scales—or feathers, depending on what light you catch it in. As you step back, closer to the light of the *Carnivale*, you draw the figure toward you. They move with the grace of a dancer, with strength and poise, wearing a grin that's decidedly wicked. They wear a hood, not unlike that of the red witch, though it reveals more because of the mask—which is a hard thing to believe. Their hair remains mostly hidden, though you see hints of its gold also reflected in eyes that might, in fact, be green. They're the only feature clearly visible under the mask, unmistakable deep, soulful, dangerous. Look too long into those eyes, you might forget even that you have eyes of your own. They wield those eyes like a mesmerist, pressing closer to you even as you retreat toward the light, pushing their advantage, hypnotizing you in the most subtle of ways. It may be too late, that you've realized this, but then you're in the glow of festival again, and the partygoers dance so closely to your back you feel them, the breath of them, the wind of their rhythmic movements, the sway of their undulating. And you realize all the people under all their masks are, in fact, in thrall to your would-be paramour, moving to a rhythm generated by those incredible, impossible eyes.

You look back at those advancing eyes and lips, that lithe body that might belong to anyone, those hands reaching out to stroke your porcelain cheek, those legs long enough to close the distance separating you even when matching your backwards scramble step for step. You look left and right, but there's no sign of your guide, who moments ago had promised to be waiting just on the other side of the light.

"You should dance with me," they say, reaching for your hand. "Ask me to dance, I don't mind. I know every step, every rhythm ever dreamed, every spin, every throw, every pirouette, every stolen embrace. The music is picking up, faster and faster, just like the beat of your heart, won't you just take my hand and give in to all the night offers?"

Your guide warned you not to agree to anything—surely a dance, whether a minuet or mere feather steps, is an agreement of some sort, a covenant, a form of surrender. Your suitor promises nothing in return, no glory, no joy, no salvation. First, they will take your hand—their fingers already ply your palm and wrist, enticing you merely to accept their embrace—they will take your hand, then maybe in the middle of the dance steal a kiss, and next they'll have your body, your heart, and your soul.

So you turn. You break away from those eyes. You flee headlong through the revelry, knocking over dancers, spilling drinks, upsetting the makeshift band with their converted pipes and strings tied to sticks doubling as instrumentation.

You run, past the trailers you haven't yet entered, past the woman distributing champagne in glasses inspired by the shape of Marie Antoinette's assets—or maybe those of Kate Moss. Past barking dogs, angry dogs, Dobermans and the like guarding secrets of some sort that you'll never uncover. Past a woman in veils performing the Dance of Death with a smiling skeletal partner, another tango meant to ensnare you. Past the man with glass eyes, the woman whose copper rings extend her neck a foot or more into the sky, an elderly man with golden teeth, a woman with four legs, another with two heads, until finally one calls out to you and says, "Here, here, you can hide here."

You duck into the wagon of one of the freaks.

Inside, the wagon is stuffed with banners proclaiming Cleo, the Moon Girl, and showing an illustration of a woman wearing almost nothing seated on the edge of a grinning sickle moon. Other banners announce the Snake Dancer, the Snake Charmer, or the Snake Girl. All of them picture the same girl—the woman before you but thirty, forty years in the past. She's older now, pale as the moon, but beautiful.

She smiles demurely, sits on one of the overly lush lounges, and says nothing. Together, you listen to the sounds of pursuit outside her tent. It's dark, but she lights a candle, a single flickering flame, though she doesn't seem to need it herself.

When you open your mouth to speak, she puts a finger to her lips to shush you.

"Here," she says, her voice a whisper as she approaches you. She reaches around the sides of your face and unfastens the porcelain mask. It comes free easily, but you see traces of blood on the inside. You reach to touch your face, but she catches your hand. "Allow me." She already has a basin filled with warm water and a towel, as though she knew you were coming. She pats at your face, at the wounds you can't even confirm are there. The cloth was white but comes away with little bits of red and pink.

Someone knocks twice on the door and pushes it open: a broad, squat gentleman in a brilliant golden mask that seems to have borrowed from stars and suns and moons and peacocks. He averts his eyes, his whole face, so as not to look directly at you or the Moon Girl, and says in a voice like rust and grease, "We seem to have a runaway."

"Well, we do hope you find them," Cleo says.

The man nods, agreeing wholeheartedly. "You might want to lock your door for the night," he says.

"I'll do no such thing, and you know it."

He nods again. He pulls the door shut and disappears.

You want to ask how he didn't recognize you—though you certainly didn't recognize him—but Cleo, the Moon Girl, holds up the porcelain mask you'd been wearing. She says, "Moonlight can play tricks, especially if you've been imbibing."

She hands the mask to you, and briefly seems reluctant to let go. "Smash it when you can," she says, "but not here, where I sleep. If you infect my nightmares with that poison, I'll come after you with all the fury of Artemis and Cynthia and Selene and Changxi and Metztli. I'll devour your soul, and my teeth can be very, very sharp." She clicks them together a few times to prove this. Her eyes are a fiery green gold, not unlike those of the dance partner you spurned.

"You'll have to run," she tells you. "They will haunt you and hound you from now till eternity, they will draw you into their horrific little carnival, they will put you to work, and if you're lucky only on the midway, if you wake before you exit those gates. You remember the gates, don't you?"

You ask, "Why are you helping me?"

She looks wistfully at one of the posters, one above all others, perhaps the oldest, the realest, the most disintegrated. "You haven't got time for my story," she says. "Did you feel that? Just a moment ago, the moon has set. You are at risk with the Sebastien Brothers. You were never safe. The sun will rise in just a few minutes. The sky already betrays the colors of today, and they're harsh colors, vibrant but stark, bright and blinding." She pushes you toward her door. "Go," she says. "Be swift."

You're back in the middle of the freaks' trailers. They stare at you: the armless painter, the spider woman, the elephantine philosopher, the rat speaker and the snake charmer, the hanged man who walks on his hands and wears a noose as a necktie, the sword swallower and the lobster boy, the human skeleton, the strongman, the albino, the twins, the puppeteer and the headless body, even the devil boy with red scales instead of skin and horns in his head. They stare because in their world, you are the freak, and you have no business being there, but at least they're not partaking in the chase. If they wanted you, they wouldn't hand you over to the true freaks in their *Carnivale* masks.

So you run. Into the maze of mirrors and glass, through the shattered pane, the shards and echoes of yourself. Without a guide, you're left to move on instinct. You feel the breath of the bull, the scrape of its hooves in the sawdust, the tinkling of glass bells. You're squeezed by one mirror, stretched by another, scattered by a third—but you keep going. There's no mirth in the grins of your reflections. There's no joy and no hope, and it's all so blatantly a trick of the mirrors. You escape, again, by crashing through the final pane of a dead end. There are no wrong turns in the mirror maze when you're in control.

You run. Back toward the corn maze, because you have to return through every level of the carnival to get to the gates through which you entered. You run, trying to duplicate your steps, not getting too close to the pumpkins, avoiding the caretakers of the corn, abruptly changing direction when you find the clowns.

Then back to the funhouse, to the room full of darkness—but with the moonlight in your eyes, you can see it's all Styrofoam mop heads and velvet curtains. You keep your feet as you pass over unsteady, uneven, and shifting floors.

On the other side, you pass the ghost tour. Jerry's still on the roof, but instead of waving, his hands are on his hips. Innumerable ghosts and spirits pace behind him like hungry tigers, a riotous mob just begging for release. When he sees you, he sticks a small gold whistle between his lips. When he blows, you don't hear it, but the ghosts most certainly do. They erupt from the ghost tour like a swarm, the sounds of chains and moans accompanying them.

Then the roller coaster, still racing, still screaming, still delighting and devouring its patrons with reckless abandon.

Then you're at the tent of the red witch, the ghosts on your heels, porcelain masks in your shadows, clowns invading your peripheral vision. You can't run, not that quickly—maybe you can hide in the red witch's cemetery. But when you throw open the flap of her tent, there's merely the inside of a tent: a small space with two chairs around a table, a crystal ball atop it, a variety of scarves and wisps of incense, and a woman enshrouded within a hooded cloak so deep a blue it's probably indigo.

She looks up at you, those eyes blue like crystals. It's not the red witch at all, but her sister.

She smiles. You can't see the smile through the shadows, but you feel it, and it doesn't feel good. It's dry, crisp, arid, coming away in flakes at the edges. She says, "You know the cost."

You have one last silver dollar in your pocket. Either you pay it, or you take your chances outside the tent where the ghosts can see you, where the clowns can smell you, where the masks can track you by the rhythm of your pulse. You withdraw the coin. She points to a gravestone inside the tent, the only one, perhaps the same as earlier, with the uneven top. Again, when you place the coin the granite bites you, drawing a trickle of blood that splashes on the coin, the stone, even the floor of the tent.

She holds a withered hand over the crystal ball and gazes into it. "Sit," she says. You hesitate only briefly. "I hate to always have to deliver bad news," she says, "but I don't see much future for you at all."

When you start to rise to your feet, she grabs your wrist. Her hand is like a hammer, like a razor blade, like a drum made of dried human flesh. "Don't be so hasty. I have words still. Allow an old woman the chance to catch her breath." Indeed, her words come slowly. She takes a breath, a deep inhalation, and when she lets it out it's a plume of cinnamon and vanilla incense covering an under-stench of rot. Her teeth look almost as blue as her garments. "You've seen my sister, and all—no, most—of what she's said has come to pass, has it not?" It's a rhetorical question. She doesn't give you time to answer. "There's still the bargain. That's what decides. Do you understand me?"

Maybe you do, maybe you don't. She releases your hand, lowers her head, and says, "You're running out of time. The sun rises. You're lucky the trees are so tall in the east, or it might already cast its rays on the carnival, and where would you be then, ha!"

Outside the dark and dusty canvas tent, you find no *Carnivale* masks, no ghosts, no clowns, no patrons or carnies, no one and nothing moving through the skeletal pre-dawn glow of the carnival. Only your guide, leaning against a pole, staring in your direction and grinning broadly.

PART FIVE

I thought I'd find you here, seeking solace from the old woman as though that's the sort of thing she deals in. She's probably sold you lies. It's her stock, her trade, her line. Ah, but it wasn't the red witch you saw this time, but her sister, her elder sister, even if only by three minutes. Age is power.

Well, we've hardly had time to show you all the secrets of the Night Carnival. You didn't even get to meet the Sebastien Brothers, or what's left of them. Their mummified remains travel with us, you see, as a kind of good luck token. You need luck in this kind of business. Good or bad, it's luck that keeps us moving, keeps us vital, keeps us alive.

Isn't the Ferris wheel grand in the last minutes of the night? Like bones, and gondolas that might carry you down sacred rivers, even rivers of moonlight. I'm sorry to say, I can't see the moon anymore. I thought she'd be with us through the night, but that's not always the case. Anyhow, the sun will crest the horizon in just a few moments, and also you'll probably awaken any moment, who can say how much time has passed in your sleep, and I haven't even shown you the most important part, the very reason you're here, the reason I've been giving you this little tour.

Here, past the Tea Cups, the Tilt-a-Whirl, the Thunder Bolt, in that plain wooden building. It's part of the grounds. We make use of it, but we won't be striking it down today, won't be carrying it off to our next destination. Just be wary of the scorpions. They tend to hide on the underside of tables, at the feet of benches and stools, wherever they can best maintain invisibility until they decide to strike.

No, it won't take but a minute. There's no hurry. It's merely an offer. A contract, you might say. No, it's not long, here, look at this. Thirteen paragraphs, the typical subsections, you agree to perform, to a share of the proceeds. No, of course it doesn't specify the act. You'll be put to work where we need you.

Stop fidgeting. I won't let you leave until you've at least considered the offer. It's not forever, not an eternity, it's not like we're trying to trap your soul here. It's an exchange, really. Some of the performers, except maybe the clowns, get tired of life and death on the road. The dust of deserts, the icy rains of winter, the spiteful epitaphs. Loves come and go, but the carnival is family, and family is in the blood. It's in your blood, even if you don't know it. Somewhere along the line, you share lineage with the Sebastien Brothers. Maybe a distant cousin, a great-great-uncle three times removed, I'm sure there's a chart of the tree in one of the cabinets. They want to put you in line to inherit.

Understand, this doesn't make the Night Carnival yours immediately, and it doesn't make any of the carnies, players, or performers part of your personal entourage. It's a line of succession, and if you read the fine print, there, buried in the fifth paragraph, you'll see you're not even next. It would require a string of devious murders to make the carnival yours after only a single night, and there's much to learn. You should know how to raise tents, how to disassemble and reassemble the Ferris wheel, how to wrap the chains, how to light the neon. We'll be teaching you the secrets of the carnival, the mysteries, the passions. We'll show you the crypts in the mother country, the king's flowers that grow only on the graves of our truest royalties. You'll dance with shadows, sing with demons, and cultivate your own geranium. You'll nurture a thousand spiders and wrangle your own additions to the livestock, maybe a shrunken-headed goat, maybe a twenty foot gator descended from Old Joe himself, or the swiftest of the wild horses from the Namib. I wouldn't put anything past you.

You haven't finished reading. Look, we'll provided food, water, wine, whiskey, and when it becomes necessary, we'll make sure you've got a pair of Colt Peacemakers, which are standard issue. You'll earn back the silver dollars you handed over to the witches and more. And every night, as you walk the carnival grounds, you'll do so hand in hand with the moon, the moon goddess, the moon girl, whoever's attention you happen to attract. She'll tell you stories of the Sebastien Brothers in the early days. You know, they inherited the carnival, too. It takes a strong personality and a lot of effort to change the name of a traveling show of any sort. Maybe one day it'll be yours, not just by contract and covenant, but body and soul. Yes, the carnival has a soul, and I am its representative. And yes, you were selected for reasons I couldn't begin to enunciate. I'm merely an emissary, a carrier of letters, a messenger of sorts—in addition to being your guide.

Don't get up. We're not done. Did you read this paragraph, here, which explains the rituals? It's a long paragraph, but hardly comprehensive. You'll learn all of them, in much greater detail, as we travel highways of dreams and legends. We'll be passing soon through Paris, I'm sure you've always wanted to see that city in all its lights, and also Shanghai, and you'll regret missing the salt cathedral.

I said, don't get up.

Don't make me chase you.

I'm not much of a runner, you see, but I do have friends.

Yes, see, you're surrounded now. Ghosts on one side, masks on the other, and I'm sure you'll hear the telltale clockworks of the clowns when they get close enough. If I were you, I'd sign the contract before the sun breaks the horizon. You have less than a minute—or we'll just put you to work, and I don't think you'll like that near as much.

PART SIX

Ghosts to your right, your guide behind you, and masks to your left between you and the midway and, ultimately, the gate. There's only one thing to do. You raise the mask, the porcelain mask that stole a bit of your blood, that attracted all of the *Carnivale* in the first place, and smash it against a random pole holding up some portion of the Night Carnival.

It shatters, spilling light and blood, screams and laughter, shadows and mist. The ghosts laugh in silence, but the revelers, whether their masks are porcelain, leather, or bone, crack at the edges of themselves, spilling more light, more screams, more mist.

So when you run—you knew it would come to that—you run through the throng, and not one can lift a finger to stop you. Even the one whose golden eyes had nearly led you astray. Even the woman who had been pouring champagne.

You run down the center of the midway, halfway between kiosks on one side or the other, games of chance, challenges of skill, tents that have now gone quiet but earlier sold candied apples and other sweets. The ghosts are like a river behind you, crashing through the carnival, overturning rings and bottles and duckies and softballs and oversized dice. The ghosts themselves are silent, but their stampede roars downhill like thunder and pulls the entirety of the carnival with them.

In the east, the very edge of the sun is almost visible through the trees. The long dawn stretches past its breaking point. The sun will rise. The day will start. The dream will end.

Ahead of you, standing in the mouth of the gate, your tall and gaunt guide awaits. He grins. He tilts his head to one side as if curious and nothing more. He slowly shakes his head.

But you rush forward anyway. When he tries to stop you, to catch you, to trip you up even if just for the second it'll take for the sun to crest the eastern sky, you pull the knife. Steel, sharp, hand carved— it had been made by a fierce woman in Colorado and previously been used to kill just one man, whether he deserved it or not. It slips easily out of its sheath. The blade glints. Slips easily into flesh. Whether you're justified or not, you feel immensely so—and you wield it in self-defense, no one can ever doubt that.

Your guide crumbles away to dust as you pass under the gate. The sun breaks the horizon. The ghosts dissolve in that first light, and the carnival is struck down—to make ready for its next destination, whether that be Paris, Tokyo, the salt cathedral, El Paso, or Boise.

And it's a dream, probably, from which you'll eventually wake. But after that happens, you'll still wonder about the Cleo, the Moon Girl, and you'll still look fearfully at clowns wherever you see them, and you'll maybe never want to walk a maze through fields of corn again. You lost the knife, having buried it in a soft spot on your guide's body, but on waking, you'll find you still have the red witch's card, *Thief*, which features an exaggerated art nouveau pickpocket displaying a wallet as he walks away from a pair of gentlemen descending, unaware, deeper into the card.

ACKNOWLEDGMENTS

I wrote this tale during the earliest and darkest months of the pandemic while hiding from the world at my sister's house. Jeneine, her husband Chuck, and her son Jacob ("The Baritone") were good enough to give me space to work on this and other projects while the world outside our doors ended.

I must also thank Ray Bradbury, whose influence I think is plainly visible throughout this story. For a long time, I didn't name him as a foundational influence on me and my writing, and lately I've begun to recognize my error.

As always, a special thanks to Sabine and the Rose Fairy. You will always be with me.

ABOUT THE AUTHOR

John Urbancik has never worked in a carnival, but in his soul he's always been a traveler.

In addition to books of poetry and photography, and a nonfiction book based on the 100 episode run of his podcast *Inkstains* (in turn based on his three-time year-long projects of the same name), Urbancik (pronounced Urban as in City, Sick as in Puppy) has written books like the *DarkWalker* series, *Stale Reality* (also available in Russian), and *Once Upon a Time in Midnight.*

Born on a small island in the northeast United States called Manhattan, he is currently sequestered in an undisclosed location in the woods of Pennsylvania near the Susquehanna River.

ALSO BY JOHN URBANCIK

NOVELS
Sins of Blood and Stone
Breath of the Moon
Once Upon a Time in Midnight
Stale Reality
The Corpse and the Girl from Miami
DarkWalker 1: Hunting Grounds
DarkWalker 2: Inferno
DarkWalker 3: The Deep City
DarkWalker 4: Armageddon
DarkWalker 5: Ghost Stories
DarkWalker 6: Other Realms

NOVELLAS
A Game of Colors
The Rise and Fall of Babylon (with Brian Keene)
Wings of the Butterfly
House of Shadow and Ash
Necropolis
Quicksilver
Beneath Midnight
Zombies vs. Aliens vs. Robots vs. Cowboys vs.
Ninja vs. Investment Bankers vs. Green Berets
Colette and the Tiger
Clockwork Ravens

COLLECTIONS
Shadows, Legends & Secrets
Sound and Vision
Tales of the Fantastic and the Phantasmagoric

POETRY
John the Revelator
Odyssey

NONFICTION
InkStained: On Creativity, Writing, and Art

INKSTAINS
Multiple volumes

www.ingramcontent.com/pod-product-compliance
Lightning Source LLC
Chambersburg PA
CBHW050833180626
46814CB00004B/1601

* 9 7 8 1 9 5 1 5 2 2 0 5 6 *